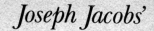

Joseph Jacobs'

The Story of the

THREE
LITTLE PIGS

Illustrated by Lorinda Bryan Cauley

G.P. PUTNAM'S SONS · NEW YORK

Illustrations copyright © 1980 by Lorinda Bryan Cauley
All rights reserved. Published simultaneously in Canada
by Academic Press Canada Limited, Toronto.
Printed in the United States of America.
First impression.
Library of Congress Cataloging in Publication Data
Three little pigs.
The story of the three little pigs.
Summary: Rather than suffer the fate of his
two brothers, a pig cleverly outwits a persistent
wolf once and for all.
[1. Folklore—England] I. Jacobs, Joseph, 1854–1916.
II. Cauley, Lorinda Bryan, III. Title.
PZ8.1.T383 1980. 398.24'529734 [E] 79-28422
ISBN 0-399-20733-3
ISBN 0-399-20732-5 pbk.
First Peppercorn paperback edition published in 1980.

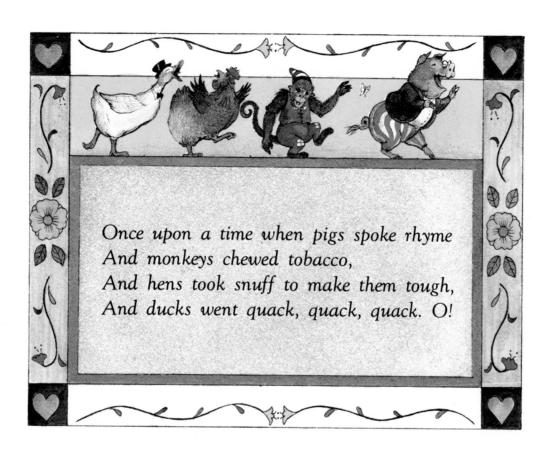

Once upon a time when pigs spoke rhyme
And monkeys chewed tobacco,
And hens took snuff to make them tough,
And ducks went quack, quack, quack. O!

There was an old sow with three little pigs, and as she had not enough to keep them, she sent them out to seek their fortune.

The first that went off met a man with a bundle
of straw, and said to him:

"Please, man, give me that straw to build me a
house."

Which the man did, and the little pig built a
house with it.

Presently came along a wolf, and knocked at the
door, and said:

"Little pig, little pig, let me come in."

"*No, no, by the hair of my chiny chin chin.*"

"Then I'll huff, and I'll puff, and I'll blow your
house in."

So he huffed, and he puffed, and he blew his
house in, and ate up the little pig.

The second little pig met a man with a bundle of furze and said:

"Please, man, give me that furze to build a house."

Which the man did, and the pig built his house.

Then along came the wolf, and said:
"Little pig, little pig, let me come in."
"No, no, by the hair of my chiny chin chin."
"Then I'll huff, and I'll puff, and I'll blow your house in."

So he huffed, and he puffed, and he puffed, and he huffed, and at last he blew the house down, and he ate up the little pig.

The third little pig met a man with a load of bricks, and said:

"Please, man, give me those bricks to build a house with."

So the man gave him the bricks, and he built his
house with them.

So the wolf came, as he did to the other little pigs, and said:

"Little pig, little pig, let me come in."

"*No, no, by the hair of my chiny chin chin.*"

"Then I'll huff, and I'll puff, and I'll blow your house in."

Well, he huffed, and he puffed, and he huffed and he puffed, and he puffed and huffed; but he could *not* get the house down.

When he found that he could not, with all his huffing and puffing, blow the house down, he said:

"Little pig, I know where there is a nice field of turnips."

"Where?" said the little pig.

"Oh, in Mr. Smith's Home-Field, and if you will be ready tomorrow morning I will call for you, and we will go together, and get some for dinner."

"Very well," said the little pig, "I will be ready. What time do you mean to go?"

"Oh, at six o'clock."

Well, the little pig got up at five, and got the

turnips before the wolf came (which he did about six), who said:

"Little pig, are you ready?"

The little pig said: "Ready! I have been and come back again, and got a nice potful for dinner."

The wolf felt very angry at this, but thought that he could outwit the little pig somehow or other, so he said:

"Little pig, I know where there is a nice apple tree."

"Where?" said the pig.

"Down at Merry-Garden," replied the wolf, "and if you will not deceive me I will come for you at five o'clock tomorrow and get some apples."

Well, the little pig bustled up the next morning at four o'clock, and went off for the apples, hoping to get back before the wolf came; but he had farther to

go, and had to climb the tree, so that just as he was coming down from it, he saw the wolf coming, which, as you may suppose, frightened him very much. When the wolf came up he said:

"Little pig, what! Are you here before me? Are they nice apples?"

"Yes, very," said the little pig. "I will throw you down one." And he threw it so far, that while the wolf went to pick it up, the little pig jumped down and ran home. The next day the wolf came again, and said to the little pig:

"Little pig, there is a fair at Shanklin this afternoon, will you go?"

"Oh yes," said the pig, "I will go; what time shall you be ready?"

"At three," said the wolf. So the little pig went off before the time as usual, and got to the fair, and bought a butter-churn.

He was going home with it when he saw the wolf
coming. Now he could not tell what to do. So he
got into the churn to hide, and by so doing turned it
round, and it rolled down the hill with the pig in it,
which frightened the wolf so much, that he ran home
without going to the fair.

He went to the little pig's house and told him how frightened he had been by a great round thing which came down the hill past him. Then the little pig said:

"Hah, so I frightened you. I had been to the fair and bought a butter-churn, and when I saw you, I got into it, and rolled down the hill."

Then the wolf was very angry indeed, and declared he *would* eat up the little pig, and that he would get down the chimney after him.

When the little pig saw what he was about, he filled his pot full of water, and made up a blazing fire. Just as the wolf was coming down, he took off the cover, and in fell the wolf. The little pig put the cover on again in an instant, boiled him up, and ate him for supper,

and lived happy ever afterwards.

On Hanukkah

On Hanukkah

BY CATHY GOLDBERG FISHMAN

ILLUSTRATED BY MELANIE W. HALL

Aladdin Paperbacks

New York   London   Toronto   Sydney   Singapore

First Aladdin Paperbacks edition October 2001

Text copyright ©1998 by Cathy Goldberg Fishman
Illustrations copyright ©1998 by Melanie W. Hall

Aladdin Paperbacks
An imprint of Simon & Schuster
Children's Publishing Division
1230 Avenue of the Americas
New York, NY 10020

Also available in an Atheneum Books for Young Readers hardcover edition.

Designed by Nina Barnett.

The text of this book is set in Novarese.
The illustrations are rendered in collagraph and mixed media.

Printed in Hong Kong
2 4 6 8 10 9 7 5 3 1

The Library of Congress has cataloged the hardcover edition as follows:
On Hanukkah / by Cathy Goldberg Fishman ; illustrated by Melanie W. Hall.—1st ed.
p. cm.
ISBN 0-689-80643-4
1. Hanukkah—Juvenile literature. I. Hall, Melanie W., ill. II. Title.
BM695.H3F57   1998
296.4'35—dc20
96-44696
ISBN 0-689-84579-0 (Aladdin pbk.)

For my mother, Peggy Fox Goldberg,
with thanks for all of the light that she has given.
—C. G. F.

For Hermine, who appreciates the magic of art.
—M. W. H.

I hold the door open wide and watch as my father takes a box out of the closet. He pulls out little tops called *dreidels* and boxes of small, brightly colored candles. He pulls out the nine-branched candlesticks called *menorahs* or *hanukkiahs*.

It is the evening before the twenty-fifth day of the Hebrew month of *Kislev*. It is time for the eight-day Jewish holiday of Hanukkah, the Festival of Lights.

On this first night of Hanukkah, I say the
Hanukkah blessings and kindle one candle on
my menorah with the helper candle, called the
shammash.

We do not blow these candles out. We let them
burn and shine in a window so everyone can see
a light in the darkness.

"Come and look!" my brother calls, pointing out a frosty window.

We crowd around him to see a crescent moon in a cold, dark sky.

"This is the time of year when the days grow shorter and shorter. And it is the time of month when the moon grows smaller and smaller," Mother says.

"Think how it must have looked in ancient Israel, over two thousand years ago, when Syrian soldiers captured the Holy Temple and put out the eternal light of the great menorah."

I think of how dark it must have been without
that light. I think of the Jewish people who fought
for many years to rededicate the Temple and bring
the light back.

On the second night of Hanukkah, I say the
Hanukkah blessings and kindle two candles with
the shammash.

We put the menorahs in a window to be a
light of hope in the darkness.

My sisters hang our Hanukkah quilt on the wall.
"That looks great!" my brother says.

We all look at the designs on the quilt. We see
menorahs and candles and dreidels and other
things that remind us of Hanukkah. Every year we
each decorate a square of the quilt.

"There is the menorah I made last year," my
sister says.

"This year I'm going to make Judah Maccabee,"
I say as I cut out fabric scraps.

I make him look strong and bright because my father says Judah Maccabee was a light to the Jewish people. With him as their leader, they were strong enough to fight the Syrian soldiers and win.

On the third night of Hanukkah, I say the Hanukkah blessings and kindle three candles with the shammash. We put the menorahs in a window to be a light of strength in the darkness.

Every Hanukkah Grandmother reads us stories.

"Read about Hannah and her seven sons," my brother pleads, "and how they wouldn't bow down to King Antiochus."

"Read about Judith," my sisters say, "and how brave she was to trick General Holofernes."

So my grandmother does. Then she reads about the great menorah in the Temple.

"When the Jews recaptured the Temple and it was repaired and cleaned," Grandmother says, "everyone wanted to make sure the light in the great menorah would never go out again. But they found only enough special oil to burn for one day. They lit the menorah and watched in amazement as the flame burned brightly for eight days, long enough to find more oil.

"The eight days were declared a holiday for all generations. Every year at this time we light menorahs in the synagogues and in our homes to remember the miracle of Hanukkah."

On the fourth night of Hanukkah, I say the Hanukkah blessings and kindle four candles on my menorah with the shammash. We put the menorahs in a window to be a light of faith in the darkness.

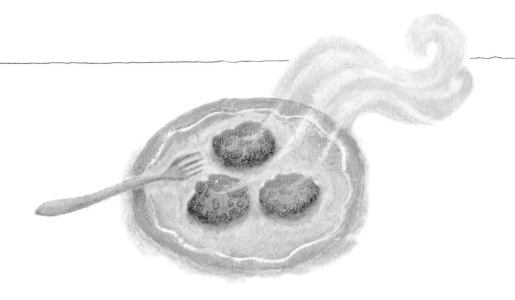

Father swings my little brother up in his arms as we go into the kitchen.

"Time to make potato *latkes*," he calls.

"Hurray!" my brother shouts.

We scrub and grate the potatoes; Mother adds eggs and onions. Then Father drops spoonfuls of the mixture into hot oil. As I watch the latkes sizzle, I think about the oil in the great menorah that burned so brightly. I think about how happy the Jews must have been to get their Temple back.

On the fifth night of Hanukkah, I say the Hanukkah blessings and kindle five candles with the shammash. We put the menorahs in a window to be a light of happiness in the darkness.

Each Hanukkah night we give presents to each other. This year I made all of the gifts I am giving. I get presents, too. Sometimes I get toys or books. Sometimes I get coins made out of chocolate or even real money. My grandfather calls it Hanukkah *gelt*. As we open our gifts, I think I would like it to be Hanukkah every night.

On the sixth night of Hanukkah, I say the Hanukkah blessings and kindle six candles with the shammash. We put the menorahs in a window to be a light of giving in the darkness.

"Who wants to play dreidel?" asks Grandfather.
"I do! I do!" we all shout.

I twist my dreidel hard with my finger and thumb, spinning it around and around. I think of the many generations of Jewish people who have played this game.

"Sometimes," Grandfather says, "we couldn't celebrate our religion or read our holy books. Jews who did not want the light of our knowledge to be lost would still get together and study. They played the game of dreidel to disguise what they were doing."

On the seventh night of Hanukkah, I say the Hanukkah blessings and kindle seven candles with the shammash. We put the menorahs in a window to be a light of knowledge in the darkness.

Grandmother plays a happy song on the piano.
We dance in a circle, spinning like dreidels,
clapping hands. Our faces glow and our eyes
shine as we sing, "O Hanukkah, O Hanukkah,
a time to remember."

As I dance I remember the story of Hanukkah,
a time when we fought for religious freedom,
won, and danced for joy.

On the eighth night of Hanukkah, I say the
Hanukkah blessings and kindle eight candles
with the shammash. We put the menorahs in a
window so everyone can see a light of freedom
in the darkness.

As we stand together on this last night, I think
each of us looks like a shining candle in the
menorah of our family. I think of each family
lighting Hanukkah candles tonight as a shining
candle in the menorah of the Jewish religion.

And I know the great menorah in the Holy Temple didn't burn for just eight days. It has burned in our hearts for over two thousand years, and that is the real miracle of Hanukkah.

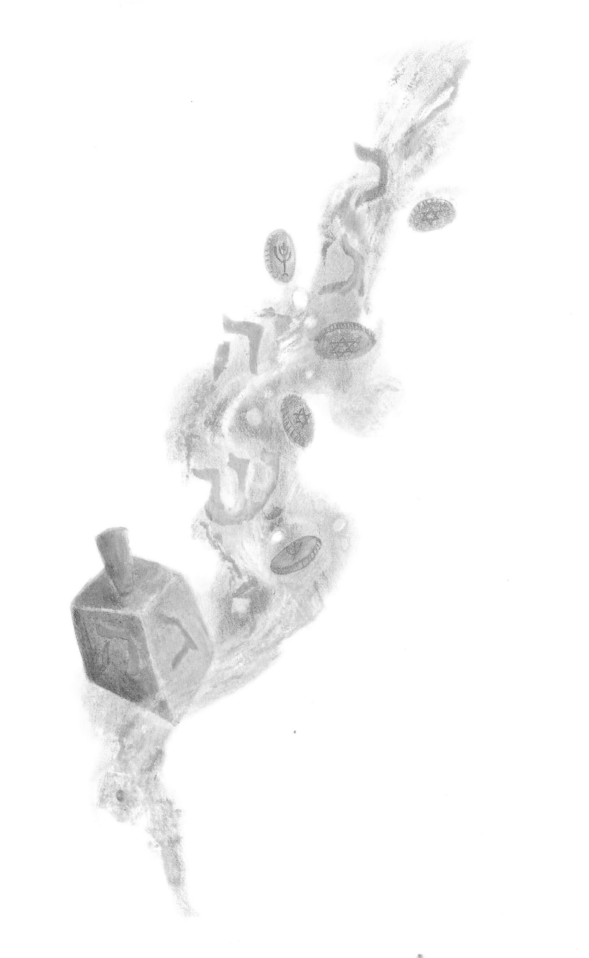

 # GLOSSARY

dreidel (DRAY dul): A spinning top with four sides. Each side is labeled with a Hebrew letter.

gelt (GEHLT): The Yiddish word for money. Yiddish is a mixture of the German and Hebrew languages, spoken by many Jews who came from Eastern Europe.

General Holofernes (ho lo FUR nais): The chief captain of the Syrian army.

hanukkiah (khah noo kee YAH): The modern Hebrew name for a Hanukkah menorah.

King Antiochus (ahn tee UH kus): the Syrian king (175–163 B.C.E.) who captured the Holy Temple and forbade the Jews to follow their religious customs.

Kislev (KISS lev): The ninth month of the ancient Hebrew calendar. It corresponds to November/December.

latke (LAT kuh): A potato pancake fried in oil and commonly served during Hanukkah.

menorah (meh NOR ah): A candelabrum. Menorahs with nine branches are used for Hanukkah. Menorahs with seven branches were used in the Holy Temple and are used in synagogues today.

shammash (SHAH mahsh): The candle, usually in the middle of the menorah, that is always lit first and is used to light all of the other candles. It is often called the helper candle.